LET'S LEARN ABOUT FOOD

VEGETABLES

Samantha Nugent

LET'S READ
AV2 BY WEIGL
ADDED VALUE · AUDIO VISUAL

www.av2books.com

LET'S READ
AV2
BY WEIGL™
ADDED VALUE • AUDIO VISUAL

Go to **www.av2books.com**, and enter this book's unique code.

BOOK CODE

Z 6 6 9 2 2 6

AV² by Weigl brings you media enhanced books that support active learning.

AV² provides enriched content that supplements and complements this book. Weigl's AV² books strive to create inspired learning and engage young minds in a total learning experience.

Your AV² Media Enhanced books come alive with...

Audio
Listen to sections of the book read aloud.

Key Words
Study vocabulary, and complete a matching word activity.

Video
Watch informative video clips.

Quizzes
Test your knowledge.

Embedded Weblinks
Gain additional information for research.

Slide Show
View images and captions, and prepare a presentation.

Try This!
Complete activities and hands-on experiments.

... and much, much more!

Published by AV² by Weigl
350 5th Avenue, 59th Floor
New York, NY 10118

Website: www.av2books.com

Library of Congress Control Number: 2015937777

ISBN 978-1-4896-4003-1 (hardcover)
ISBN 978-1-4896-4004-8 (soft cover)
ISBN 978-1-4896-4005-5 (single user eBook)
ISBN 978-1-4896-4006-2 (multi-user eBook)

Printed in the United States of America in Brainerd, Minnesota
1 2 3 4 5 6 7 8 9 0 19 18 17 16 15

062015
160615

Editor: Katie Gillespie   Designer: Mandy Christiansen

Weigl acknowledges Getty Images, iStock, Corbis, and Dreamstime as the primary image suppliers for this title.

VEGETABLES

CONTENTS

2 AV² Book Code
4 All Kinds of Vegetables
6 Where Do Vegetables Come From?
8 What Do Vegetables Taste Like?
10 Caring for Plants
12 Choosing Vegetables
14 Vegetables in My Country
16 Enjoying Vegetables
18 Healthy Bodies
20 Keeping Clean
22 Have a Vegetable Party
24 Key Words/Log on to www.av2books.com

I like to eat vegetables. Vegetables come in many different shapes, sizes, and colors.

5

Vegetables come from plants. Some vegetables grow above the ground. Other vegetables grow under the ground.

Broccoli comes from the stem and flowers of a plant.

Vegetables can feel crunchy or soft. Some vegetables taste sweet. Other vegetables taste bitter.

I like to eat vegetables at meals and at snack time. Sometimes, I drink vegetable juice.

Farmers give plants plenty of water. This helps the plants to grow and make vegetables.

Plants also need soil, air, and sunshine to grow.

Farmers care for vegetables until they are picked. Trucks take the vegetables away when they are ready to eat.

I help choose my vegetables at the grocery store and the farmer's market. Sometimes, I choose frozen vegetables or vegetables in cans.

13

14

Many kinds of vegetables grow in America. Lettuce and peas are grown where the weather is cool.

Celery and peppers grow in warm places.

Many foods have vegetables in them. Potato chips and soup can both be made with vegetables.

I like to eat foods made with vegetables.

I eat many different colors of vegetables to stay healthy.

Eating vegetables gives me energy to play.

It is important to make sure my vegetables are clean. I wash my vegetables with water before I eat them.

I wash my hands with soap and warm water before I eat. I sing *Happy Birthday* two times to make sure I have scrubbed long enough.

21

How to Make Ants on a Log

Vegetables are even better when you share them with your friends and family. Enjoy your ants on a log at snack time. This recipe makes enough for five servings.

You will need:

- an adult
- kitchen sink
- 1 dish towel
- 1 knife
- 1 cutting board

- 1 spoon
- 5 stalks of celery
- 1/2 cup (118 milliliters) of peanut butter
- 1/4 cup (59 ml) of raisins

Directions

1. Wash your hands with soap and warm water.

2. Run the celery under cold water and dry it with a clean dish towel.

3. Have an adult help cut the celery stalks in half and remove the leaves.

4. Use the spoon to spread peanut butter into the hollow part of the celery.

5. Place raisins on top of each piece of celery so they look like ants sitting on a log.

6. Refrigerate any leftover celery.

7. Share your ants on a log snack with your friends and enjoy!

KEY WORDS

Research has shown that as much as 65 percent of all written material published in English is made up of 300 words. These 300 words cannot be taught using pictures or learned by sounding them out. They must be recognized by sight. This book contains 61 common sight words to help young readers improve their reading fluency and comprehension. This book also teaches young readers several important content words, such as proper nouns. These words are paired with pictures to aid in learning and improve understanding.

Page	Sight Words First Appearance
4	and, come, different, eat, I, in, like, many, to
7	a, above, from, grow, of, other, plants, some, the, under
8	at, can, or, sometimes, time
11	air, also, give, helps, make, need, this, water
12	are, away, for, my, take, they, until, when
15	America, is, kinds, places, where
16	be, both, foods, have, made, them, with
19	me, play
20	before, enough, hands, important, it, long, two

Page	Content Words First Appearance
4	colors, shapes, sizes, vegetables
7	broccoli, flowers, ground, stem
8	juice, meals
11	farmers, soil, sunshine
12	cans, farmer's market, grocery store, trucks
15	celery, lettuce, peas, peppers
16	potato chips, soup
19	energy
20	*Happy Birthday*, soap

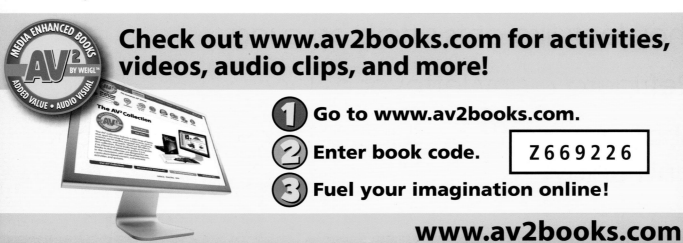